GOOD
NIGHT

This book belongs to:

Wyatt and Kate

Wishing you sweet dreams.
Makell♡

SWEET
DREAMS

Good Night, Sweet Dreams

By Makell Moody

Illustrated by Manny Aguiler

JongTale PUBLISHING

Good Night, Sweet Dreams
Copyright © 2020 by Makell Moody.
All rights reserved.
ISBN 978-1-941515-12-9
Library of Congress Control Number:
2020918530

Published by LongTale Publishing
www.LongTalePublishing.com
6824 Long Drive Houston, Texas 77087

LongTale® is a registered trademark
of LongTale Publishing.

Illustrations by Manny Aguiler

Design by Monica Thomas for
TLC Book Design, *www.TLCBookDesign.com*

In-house editor: Sharon Wilkerson

Printed in Canada

To my parents and loved ones
who always supported my dreams.
I love you all.

♥ Makell

On a little farm
where the stars shined bright
lived a young girl named Emiko.
She spent most of her time
taking care of her animals.
A horse, a cow, a tiger, a lion and
an elephant slept happily inside the barn.

But not Emiko,
she was having a
nightmare.
She had nightmares
every night.

One morning, Emiko woke up
and went to the barn to say hello
and to feed all of the animals.

Each of the animals loved Emiko
so much because of her kind heart.
She loved them too.

Emiko arrived at the barn to find Kion the lion
and Lily the tiger playing with a ball of yarn.
She gave them a big piece of meat to share.

Next, she walked over to Shelly the cow.
Emiko gave Shelly a bucket of food. The cow put
her nose inside, and the bucket got stuck on her head.
Emiko giggled and helped the silly cow slip off the bucket.

After feeding all the animals inside the barn, Emiko walked into the woods to find Tiny the elephant. He was sitting next to a baby bear that Emiko had not met before. Emiko gave Tiny some peanuts and found some blueberries for the baby bear.

She named the baby bear, Honey.

When Emiko heard her parents call for her to do her chores, she said goodbye to Tiny and Honey and blew them a kiss.

Once she got back to the house,
she began her chores.
She cleaned her room.

She washed the dishes
and took out the trash.

As soon as she was finished,
she returned to the barn
to play with the animals.

Emiko stayed in the barn
until it turned dark.
The animals carried her
back to the house and
put her in bed.

That night, Emiko had a bad dream. A tornado was chasing her,
and she woke up frightened. She went to the barn to
visit the animals and told them about her nightmare.

The next day, the animals
came up with a plan.

When the stars lit up the sky that night,
they went outside and watched a
shooting star go by. They all made the
same wish...that Emiko would have
good dreams for the rest of her life.

A glowing light appeared in
front of their eyes.
When it disappeared,
there stood a creature.

The creature had
the face of an ELEPHANT,
the ears and mane of a LION,
the body of a BEAR,
feet of a TIGER,
and tail of a COW.

The strange creature,
known as a Baku,
told them its name was Bo.

Bo made his way to the house where
Emiko was asleep. He crawled through her
window and stood next to her bed.

He saw the tornado chasing her in her dream.
He began to eat the nightmare away
and replaced it with a good dream.

Suddenly, Emiko woke up. Bo had already turned into
a stuffed animal, so he could always be with her.
She hugged the animal tightly.

Her parents opened the bedroom door to check on her.
Her mother whispered GOODNIGHT and
her father said SWEET DREAMS.

All of the barn animals were happy that their wish had come true and they were able to help Emiko.

That night, the whole farm
slept with nothing but
sweet dreams.

MAKELL MOODY is a graduate of St. Pius X High School in Houston, Texas. When she was in the fourth grade, she had nightmares every night and was afraid to fall asleep. While growing up, she had loved learning about all kinds of mythology and came across the legend of the Baku. This creature, said to devour nightmares, helped Makell overcome her fear. She sewed together her own stuffed animal to match the Baku in the legend. Later, she wrote this story in hopes that it would give other children something to help them overcome their nightmares and sleep peacefully. She is currently a sophomore, majoring in English, at Texas Christian University in Fort Worth, Texas.